Ellie McDoodle

HAVE PEN, WILL TRAVEL

Books by Ruth McNally Barshaw

Ellie McDoodle: Have Pen, Will Travel

Ellie McDoodle: New Kid in School

Ellie McDoodle: Best Friends Fur-Ever

Ellie McDoodle: Most Valuable Player

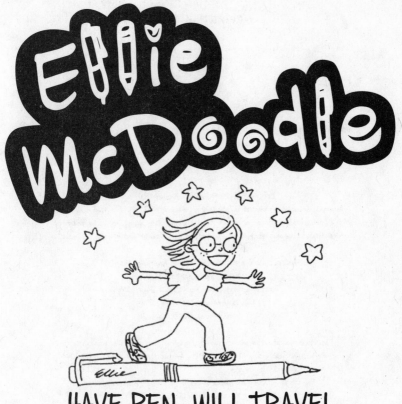

Ellie McDoodle

HAVE PEN, WILL TRAVEL

WRITTEN AND ILLUSTRATED BY

Ruth McNally Barshaw

BLOOMSBURY

NEW YORK BERLIN LONDON SYDNEY

Dedicated to those who bring
imagination to life.

First published in the United States of America in May 2007
by Bloomsbury Books for Young Readers
First paperback edition published in June 2008
This edition published in May 2011
www.bloomsburykids.com

For information about permission to reproduce selections from this book, write to
Permissions, Bloomsbury BFYR, 175 Fifth Avenue, New York, New York 10010

The Library of Congress has cataloged the hardcover edition as follows:
Barshaw, Ruth McNally.
Ellie McDoodle : have pen, will travel / by Ruth McNally Barshaw.—1st U.S. ed.
p.   cm.
Summary: Eleven-year-old Ellie McDoodle illustrates her sketchbook with chronicles
of her adventures and mishaps while camping with her cousins, aunt, and uncle.
ISBN-13: 978-1-58234-745-5 • ISBN-10: 1-58234-745-X (hardcover)
[1. Camping—Fiction. 2. Cousins—Fiction. 3. Interpersonal relations—Fiction. 4. Adventure and
adventurers—Fiction.] I. Title. II. Title: Ellie McDoodle. III. Title: Have pen will travel.
PZ7.B28047El 2007   [Fic]—dc22   2006028424

ISBN 978-1-59990-715-4 (reissue)

Printed in the U.S.A. by Quad/Graphics, Fairfield, Pennsylvania
3 5 7 9 10 8 6 4 2

All papers used by Bloomsbury Publishing, Inc., are natural, recyclable products
made from wood grown in well-managed forests. The manufacturing processes
conform to the environmental regulations of the country of origin.

WARNING:

This spy sketchbook belongs to me,
Ellie* Marie McDoodle.**

DO NOT READ UNDER PENALTY OF PLAGUE & PESTILENCE!

—— No Mercy ——

* Eleanor. What can I say? My parents have bad taste in girls' names. Bad names should be illegal!

** It's really McDougal, but the kids at school call me McDoodle because that's what I love to do: draw.

Day 1 ← Wait, that is so stupid—Day 1 would be 100 million years ago when time began and it would mean nothing happened before . . . but PLENTY has happened.

THIS is the usual me.

Detail:

x-treme happiness

This is my parents racing to the airport because Dad's old uncle Peter died.

My family:

Dad and Mom are sad but happy. They get to travel and see old friends.

Risa, 17, and Josh, 14, are happy. They get to stay home without parents. Ben-Ben, 3, is happy because that's his only mood.

Why am I unhappy?

On the way to the airport, Mom and Dad dump
Ben-Ben and me at our cousins' house.
Total dread for three reasons:
1. All of the cousins are pains.

Deanna, age 11   Eric, ← her twin   Tiffie, age 7

I really, really, REALLY can't stand Eric.

2.
Aunt Mug
and Uncle
Ewing are
pains, too.

She spits
when she yells.

His neck
turns red
when he's mad.

3. Ben-Ben is a monkey boy.

He never walks, only runs and
climbs and crashes into everything.
So he always wears a crash helmet.
He ransacks my stuff.

As if that isn't bad enough, we're all going camping. With them, it's more like cramping.

My parents think this will be fun for me. They are of course delusional.

You love camping, so this will be great! See you in a week! Take care of Ben-Ben!

So now I'm trapped in a steel projectile, hurtling down the highway into the Great Unknown with a bunch of control freaks and snotty-nosed brats. Eric started a fight with Deanna and Tiffie so Aunt Mug is making me sit next to him.

I'd rather ride on the roof rack.

Our Van

Aunt Ug

Uncle Ewing

Er-ICK

Me, up to my armpits in cereal boxes (and none of it's my favorite kind)

Ben-Ben the monkey boy

Prissy Tiffie

Boring Bossy Deanna

Supplies crammed into every spare inch

Why I have this sketchbook

1. To spy. No—OBSERVE things. I'm just observing life around me. Like in science class!
2. To remember important stuff.
3. Evidence of how demented this group is.
4. It's my only hope for keeping my sanity.

My view of the nearest window:

The History of Aunt Ug

Perpetual bad mood, and science has not yet determined WHY. Her name is actually Mug, not Ug. And I would NEVER call her Aunt Ug to her face.

When she was born, my mom couldn't say Margaret, so she called her Mug and the name stuck.

I would hate to have my sister name me. She has worse ideas than my mom.

Aunt Mug

as a baby

as a kid

as a teenager

as a bride

I think she smiled once but people were so shocked they forgot to take a picture of it.

CHARACTER STUDY
Uncle Ewing, the uncle

drawn by
Ellie McDoodle
Artist
Extraordinaire

messy hair

stares off into space a lot

sense of humor (can be seen only under a micro-scope)

neck as temperature gauge (red means a storm is coming)

usually quiet

mad view   ecstatic view   nervous view

What does he like? I have no idea. I bet HE doesn't know, either!

As for Er-ick,
all I can say is that
ten minutes with him
makes my brain
scream for
mercy.

He lies, he cheats, he steals.
(Some of this I know for a fact, firsthand.)

When Aunt Ug buys a bag of cookies, he licks
every cookie so nobody else will want them. He is
a nose-picking, booger-slurping, bug-infested
parasite.

I'm saved by Aunt Ug, who FINALLY decides it's SNACK TIME.

> Take one bag and pass the rest back.

So of course Er-ick tries to take TWO bags.

Three cookies and a bunch of pretzel sticks.

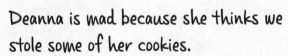

Now we're gonna be thirsty and they don't allow drinks in their van.

Deanna is mad because she thinks we stole some of her cookies.

Tiffie is whining because her bag dropped and the cookies broke.

It gets so noisy that Aunt Ug
starts a quiet contest.

What are you drawing?

SHHH!

Why?

Because it's a
quiet contest!

Is that my mom?
Did you draw my mom?

SHHH!

Is that my m—

SHHH!
Look, I'll give you
one of my cookies
if you'll be quiet.

Okay!
Also two pretzels!

What's the point of a quiet contest? There's no prize. But it's better than hearing everyone fight, I guess.

Still, it's hardly quiet.

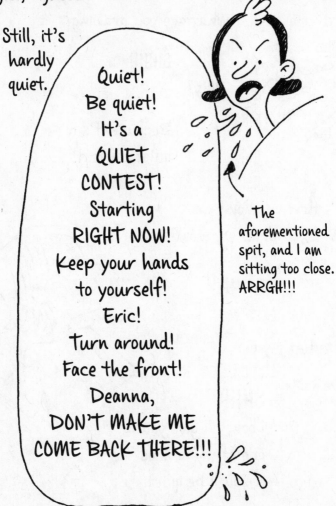

Quiet!
Be quiet!
It's a
QUIET
CONTEST!
Starting
RIGHT NOW!
Keep your hands
to yourself!
Eric!
Turn around!
Face the front!
Deanna,
DON'T MAKE ME
COME BACK THERE!!!

The aforementioned spit, and I am sitting too close. ARRGH!!!

What she really means: Don't make me come back there and spit on you!

Tiffie won the quiet contest, but there's no prize.
So she's sulking.

Cheezers. Get over it, Tiffie.
She's named after a fancy lamp, but this Tiffany
isn't too bright.

Understanding Tiffie:

> very pretty

very empty
fancy hair
fancy clothes

fancy shoes

If Tiffie were a dog
she'd be a prissy little
frou-frou show dog
all fluffed up and barky.

Yap! Yap!
Yap! Yap!
Yap! Yap!
STOP IT!!

STUFF TO DO IN THE CAR

Read

Sketch

Sleep

SPY on the enemy

Observe (it's starting to rain)

Plan time AWAY FROM these people at camp

Write notes in disappearing ink*

* I love spy supplies

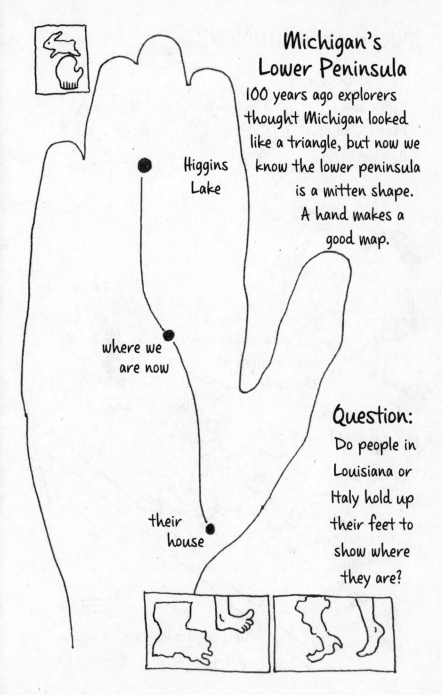

Michigan's Lower Peninsula

100 years ago explorers thought Michigan looked like a triangle, but now we know the lower peninsula is a mitten shape. A hand makes a good map.

Higgins Lake

where we are now

their house

Question:
Do people in Louisiana or Italy hold up their feet to show where they are?

Ahh, finally—LUNCH

It's pouring rain. Tiffie and I race ahead of everyone else.

Pick a good table

Aunt Ug

Uncle Ewing makes everyone be quiet at the table.

Deanna being boring

Er-ick the icky is eating all the sugar packets

Me (spying) next to Tiffie

Feed the jukebox

I choose "High Hopes"—Dad's favorite song, where the ant keeps trying & finally succeeds.

Tiffie chooses "The Hokey Pokey"—Grandpa's favorite.

Me   Tiffie

I teach Tiffie how to draw ants on the napkins.

We both hold our pens weird, but not the same weird.

We draw faces on our hands and act out the Hokey Pokey.

"You put your right foot in . . ."

Tiffie wants me to write out all of the "High Hopes" song lyrics so she can memorize them.

Ben-Ben the crazy monkey boy runs all over the place

I wish I was home. These people are SO annoying.

Bleah.

Back in the car, and it's still raining.

I like to watch the little rivers of raindrops on the van windows and try to guess which direction they'll go. It's like they're alive.

I feel bad when they hit the window's edge. It's like they die.

Weird how you can just cross an imaginary line and the rain STOPS.   ☺

Er-ick is reading a graphic novel.
Interesting. I didn't think he could read.

You can tell you're getting close to camp by:
1. the hills on the highway
2. lots of forests
3. deer, back in the trees
4. touristy billboards

The Mystery Spot!
Mysterious!
(?) ←
North on I-75,
Exit at the big tree,
turn left at the fence

Souvenirs!
Flotsam & Jetsam
Castle of Trinkets

Every souvenir you can
imagine—and some you can't!

Fred Moose
Museum

It'll amaze and
a-moose you

I am an expert at camping. We always use tents and we've been coming to Higgins Lake since I was a baby, I guess, so I know the area really well.

These people hardly ever go camping and they're using a cabin.

Boring!

They wouldn't let me bring my own tent.

Tiffie has to go to the bathroom, and they're telling her to hold it because we're almost there and nobody wants to stop. We cross over the Au Sable River (pronounced "sahbo," NOT "saybul" like Deanna just said). Grandpa took me fishing on the Au Sable when I was four. (Tiffie's turning red.) Past the bait shop and the museum and the fish hatchery sign. (Tiffie's turning green.) FINALLY! State Park entrance. (Tiffie's eyeballs are yellow.) Check-in takes a longgggg time. At last we drive to the cabin. But Tiffie still has to run to the bathroom, six campsites away. She makes it. I go with her and tease her about ME taking the first available stall and making her wait. She cries over the dumbest things.

Cheezers.

Unpack. Assigned beds (of course).
It's a pretty small place.

woods

stacking cots we
brought with us:
Tiffie over me

bunk bed

Deanna
over
Aunt Ug
and
Ben-Ben

bunk
bed

Er-ick
over
Uncle
Ewing

door

fire pit

cereal   coolers

the
van

picnic
table

← to lake

to bathrooms
and playground →

Free time until dinner, but we have to stay near the cabin.

CHEEZERS.

If I want to get reprimanded I'll hang out with Uncle Ewing. So I LEAVE. Yell at an empty swing, Duh-anna.

Grrrrr . . .

Deanna acts like she's SO smart, like she's really mature. But she is 4 months and 17 days YOUNGER than me.

And besides, she isn't that nice either. She pulls all the heads off Tiffie's dolls and puts their clothes on backward. You call that MATURE?

Anyway, I was just playing around.

I'm outta here.

HIGGINS LAKE CAMP

I'm supposed to be the spy, but all of a sudden this kid sneaks up on me.

This is Scott from Kalamazoo.

age: just turned 13

speaks French, Japanese, and English

big, soft eyes

wears a little pouch—I'm not sure what's in it

says he can't draw but wants to learn

medic kit in pocket

camouflage pants

Scott is mysterious. I think a person could talk to him for eons and still not know everything about him.

Scott and I take a walk in the meadow and the woods. We see deer! We're very quiet and one comes within 10 feet of us. Amazing!

tree swallow—blue-green shiny bird dives and glides gracefully

honey locust tree seed pod, eaten by deer, chipmunks, and squirrels

deer trail

blue racer snake, about 3 feet long

I can't believe how much
Scott knows about nature.

The coolest things we find:

Deer bones!
They're completely
white—Scott says
that means they've
been here a while.

legs →

ribs

spine

tooth,
actual size!

We're reassembling
the skeleton. It's
like a puzzle.
This is SO COOL!

Until Deanna finds us . . .

"Oh my GOSH! You guys are SICK! Those bones are DISGUSTING! And anyway you're in trouble, Ellie. You're late for dinner, PLUS you were supposed to stay within six campsites of our cabin."

Bye, Scott! See you after dinner!

Scott's Campsite is #137.

DINNER:
Hot dogs & chili &
baked potatoes

Aunt Mug isn't a bad cook, but I want to cook my own hot dog on a stick over the fire. Predictably, they say NO.

They also say I can't go visit Scott after dinner. Er-ick keeps trying to grab this book so finally I just have to sit on it.

Eric!
No more
potato chips.

There's
none left.
:(

The girls do the dishes (boys will do breakfast).
Yippee. More time with Deanna.

She's as much of a control freak as her parents!
I get even, though.

So then I splash
her, but not very much,
and she slaps me with a wet
towel, which HURTS. Pretty soon we're both
being punished by: 1) having to do the dishes in
the morning, and 2) having to sit across from
each other for half an hour WITHOUT being mean
to each other.

I guess our grandpa used to stop fights this way
when our moms were kids. It's better than his
infamous Doorknob Punishment. (Hold your nose
against a doorknob until you're in a better mood.)

Also I wasn't allowed to work on this book for
half an hour.

Eventually I ask Deanna if she wants to play
20 Questions and she says yeah, so we do.

35

Woods

Giant
frog
pond!!

Woods

Tiny path

Tree with
long branch

Small stream with
very cold water

Lake

Woods

Beach

According to Er-ick,
a car sank in the pond 50
years ago and the driver drowned. The locals
call her Seaweed Sally, and to this day her ghost
tries to lure people into a watery, mucky grave.

Thick, deep, dark,
scummy pond.
I don't see a car or
any dead people.

Wow, Er-ick is right. I have
NEVER seen so many FROGS.
I'm drawing them (and looking at their ears)
but everyone else is catching them. I am morally
superior. Frogs don't belong in baskets and pails.

Big fat
bullfrogs, cute
little tadpoles,
teeny-tiny frogs.
They catch
DOZENS.

Of course, Aunt Ug won't let them bring the frogs inside the cabin. So they line up all the containers outside and cover the openings so the frogs can breathe but they can't escape.

So, what are you guys going to do with all those frogs?

Take 'em home as pets. Hopefully THIS time, some of them will survive.

Eventually we say good night to the frogs and go inside the cabin.

Geez. Why can't I use one tiny flashlight to work on my book?

My flashlight won't wake anyone up. His YELLING does, though.

I give up.

Good night.

Day 2

It's morning and it's raining outside. Bleah.
This is torture. Wall-to-wall relatives. After three
Quiet Contests, a half hour of forced reading
(weird how being forced to do something you love
makes you not like it), and a breakfast of their
favorite cereal but not mine, I just want OUT.

Me: Can't I go out for a walk? I have a poncho.
Them: NO.

Aunt Ug passed out pipe cleaners and told us to make things we saw at camp. I made these:

I know who that is! It's that weird guy with the purse that Smellie was talking to!

I'm Er-ick and I'm a dotty mandrill!*

*crazy baboon

Then I get a genius idea. I teach them how to play Spoons. Er-ick wins without even cheating. This is actually fun but you won't catch me admitting that to anyone here.

HOW TO PLAY 🥄🥄 (SPOONS)

It's like musical 🪑s, but with 🥄s.

Deal each 🧍 4 🃏🃏🃏.

Dealer grabs 1 🃏 from the pile,

tries to match it with the 🃏🃏🃏 in his ✋,

and passes 1 🃏 to the player on his right.

Whoever has 4 of a kind first grabs a 🥄 quietly.

When the others notice a 🥄 is gone,

they try to grab a 🥄 also.

But with 5 🧍🧍🧍🧍🧍 you play with 4 🥄🥄🥄🥄,

so someone loses. The loser gets an "S."

Then start another round. If the same 🧍 loses again he or she gets a "P" until it spells out "SPOONS" and the game ends. (Each time you play a round, a new 🧍 gets to deal the 🃏🃏🃏.)

And if you have a 👧 like Ben-Ben around, it's good to give him extra 🃏🃏🃏 so he doesn't wreck your game.

After nine rounds of Spoons, things start to get ugly again so Aunt Ug and Uncle Ewing make us go to the . . .

This is good. I can go off on my own. Lots of tourists here but I will spy on the dead animals instead.

fox —
smaller than
I expected

raccoon —
bigger than
I expected

field mouse —

Once we caught a tiny field mouse in a big box, in my dad's office. We left it for five minutes to get a better cage and when we got back the mouse had disappeared.

porcupine —
What's his favorite game?
Poker.

Meadow Muskie —

Fred Moose is famous for this fish. Now extinct, it ran on land with footprints facing opposite directions, to fool its enemies. I was 10 before I realized it was a joke.

duck
(wood)

duck
(mallard)

goose
(Canada)

bald eagle
from 1857

Bald eagles aren't bald, except on their feet.

Native American
eagle symbol

Native American symbol
for stupidity

Eagles taste like chicken! Ha ha ha!

The Fred Moose people take their moose seriously.

The drinking fountain is a moose head.

All the people
here are wearing
moose souvenirs
and giving the
    Fred Moose
antler greeting.
    I think it's goofy.

BEN-BEN
The Monkey Boy, Unleashed

Ben-Ben gets into everything as soon as you turn your back.

Totem pole goes up to the third floor

And he's always missing a sock and a shoe.

One minute Ben-Ben is hanging on the moose antlers.

The next minute he's at the top of the totem pole.

How does he do it? I repeat— he's part monkey.

A Study of Nearby Wildlife
Deanna, age 11.

dangerous talons

highly vocal:
- shrill nasal bleats
- roars when angry
- aggressive growl
- barks out orders
- whimpers when she doesn't get her way

acute vision but not a cute face

good at one thing: sports; gallops at moderate speeds.

Sometimes born in pairs: This specimen is the older of the twins by 3 minutes, and also is taller and dominant. This makes Er-ick feel unimportant, so he misbehaves.

Deanna, → dominant twin

Er-ick, inferior twin

Spying on people in the store . . .

Aunt Ug's trying to convince the younger kids they want cheap souvenirs instead of expensive ones. Tiffie gets a water bottle.

Er-ick spends his money on fake dog poop and plastic flies and of course candy.

Deanna buys a sweatband (ew) but what she really wants is the soccer ball.

Oh, Er-ick, you are SO witty.
My answers:
- Nah, he's too much of an airhead.
- He's a very well-rounded guy.
- They'd have a ball together.
- Let the good times roll!
- What would a love triangle look like?
- A year later they could have a bouncing baby boy.

Ben-Ben
was here

Uncle Ewing gets a book on astronomy.
I buy a bag of cool rocks and two books: *Survival*
and *Animal Tracks*.

Petoskey stone

quartz crystal

striped sedimentary

Outside there's a double rainbow over the town.

Back at camp . . .

While Tiffie and Ben-Ben count worms on the ground by the cabin, I'm off to show Scott the sketches I did.

I let Scott read this book. His campsite feels
more like what I'm used to. It's REAL camping.
I'm embarrassed to be staying in the cabin with
my cousins. It's too much like a hotel. I like
roughing it instead.

Scott shows me what he keeps in his bag.

deerskin pouch

shark tooth for courage

pencil stub

old Roman coin for "Learn from the past"

feather from favorite bird friend

heart-shaped rock for "Respect the earth"

mini flashlight

We walk to the lake. It's too cold to swim, but we wade on the shore.

I can tell Scott almost anything, but I don't think I can tell him that I like him.

Dinnertime back at the cabin.

Yes. That's right. Ben-Ben is eating cereal out of the box WITH HIS FEET. It's the cereal I dislike the least, too.

All the wood is wet so the cooking fire is a pillar of smoke.
Smoky canned stew filled with ash from burning newspapers. YUM.

 Plus Er-ick puts plastic flies in everyone's food.

YIKES!
Must stay calm. Every move calculated.
I can't let them get curious about my book.
They might gang up on me and try to steal it.
Must keep this book out of enemy hands! Quick—
divert their attention with a game.

Whew. Crisis averted. We play I Spy for a while
(until everyone just keeps guessing "a tree")
and then I get them to play Human Pretzel with
a bunch of other kids at the playground.

Okay, first everyone
grab hands with
two other people.

Hold on, and untangle into a big circle without letting go.

We play this four times, and each time Scott grabs my hand.

We do Fing Fang Fooey to figure out who will be "it" for the next game.

FING FANG FOOEY:
1. Everyone puts one hand in the circle.

2. Everyone says "Fing, Fang, Fooey!" while pumping their hand into the circle, and on the word "Fooey" everyone holds out 1, 2, or 3 fingers.

3. Add up all the fingers, then count around the circle starting with the youngest player. The player the number lands on becomes "it."

BLOB TAG:

"It" tries to tag someone.

When she does, they link arms & try to tag people.

Pretty soon "it" has turned into a huge blob.

It gets late and we go back to the cabin for a nice smoky campfire. Bleah.

Thanks to the rain, there are a million mosquitoes.

Double bleah.

And a zillion biting black flies. OUCH!

I go into the cabin early so I can work on my book. And when everyone else comes in to go to bed, they let in all the mosquitoes.

Ah, what a nice night.

˙‿˙

Day 3
ARRGHHH!

Tiffany
PEED
on me!!!

These stupid cots LEAK!!
And then—while carrying my stinking sleeping bag outside to air it out—I see a note!

What a find!

To Eric from ?

What a FAKE!
Er-ick planted it for me.

Smelly Ellie
You're a
LOSER
Hahaha

And now Aunt Ug's saying we have to go to the trout hatchery in town. I'm so sick of these people.

Uncle Ewing drops us off at the trout hatchery while he goes to the laundromat. Who has the tougher job? ME, I believe.

THE TROUT HATCHERY:

Stand around for hours and watch fish swim. For excitement, pay 25¢ for a handful of fish food pellets to throw into the water.

Er-ick puts a handful of fish food down my shirt, so now my back smells like rotting skunky fish.

Somehow, some way, I will get revenge. I'll ask Scott for some ideas on how to get even with Er-ick.

sand in his sleeping bag

nest of spiders in his duffel bag

Revenge, sweet revenge . . .

embarrass him

Eric likes to play with dolls.

meat in his shoes

"Please, please, Ellie, I beg of you, don't punish me anymore. I've learned my lesson. I'll do whatever you want from now on. Let me do your chores."

Back at camp, FINALLY, with a clean sleeping bag that Uncle Ewing washed. It's the least he could do. I'm off to site #137 to find my only friend at this lousy campground... ☺

Oh, NO NO NO NO NO!

tent was here

137

138

tire tracks

Scott's family is GONE!

Now I'm really alone. Maybe I'll stay here all night. Just me and the bugs.

I just can't believe Scott left without saying good-bye. I can't believe I'm stuck with these awful relatives who wet their beds and micromanage my time.

My choices:

___ Tolerate them for 4 more days.

___ Hide until it's time to go home.

___ Be straight with them and tell them I can't stand them (start a WAR).

___ Take the bus back to my house.

___ Tell a park ranger I'm lost and need to get back home by tomorrow.

___ Form an alliance with one of them so at least someone is on my side.

Prediction for the rest of this camping trip:

okay____ bad____ awful____ terrible____ horrible____ worst ever____ disaster____

Maybe Scott left a message for me somewhere. This will take some detective work.

I am sooooo relieved. Even if I don't ever call him, it's nice to know that Scott left a good-bye message for me.

I decide to leave a tribute for him. He won't ever see it, but the earth knows it's there.

The elephant symbolizes wisdom, strength, good luck, and of course, never forgetting.

This is not good.
We are eating tacos for dinner, and nobody
notices when Ben-Ben leaves the table.

Until he comes back,

holding
a frog—
the BEST frog—

way too tight.

Its guts are
oozing out.

I think this might be the very grossest thing I have seen in my whole life. And Ben-Ben has no idea what he did.

I'm gonna throw up.

Wait! Poke it! Make sure it's dead!

Okay, kids, go do something else. I need to bury it.

Uncle Ewing buries it. We make sure the rest of the frogs are okay. Aunt Ug puts dinner away and makes us get ready for a nature walk.

Be ready to go in five minutes.

May I be excused?

No.

Great.

I never get my way at home, either.

Okay, I guess this isn't too bad. We walk to the beach and skip stones across the water.
I hope it's warm enough to swim tomorrow.

I have to find a way to let the frogs go, so the rest aren't killed or forced to live in captivity!

After the lake, we all go to the playground. This part shocks me: They play tag! Mostly I just take notes.

Tiffie gets Ben-Ben or Aunt Ug

Aunt Ug gets Tiffie

Deanna always lets Ben-Ben get her

Er-ick mostly chooses his dad or the younger kids or me.

I'm surprised they are capable of playing a game together. Usually the only thing they do together is fight. Or imprison and kill frogs.

My new survival book tells how to get through hurricanes, quicksand, and tiger attacks, but it doesn't really help with my situation.

TIPS FOR SURVIVING CAMP
with relatives you can't stand

keep your distance

don't say much

don't pick up any of their bad habits

if confronted by the enemy, back away slowly

keep your eye on the prize

have a pen handy

They're done playing tag at the playground.

Hey—I have an idea! Lets go back to the cabin and play Hunka Bunka!

Huh?

What's Hunka Bunka?

It's where you play tag, but around the edges of a room. You're not allowed to touch the ground. You have to jump on the beds and dressers and stuff, and when you get to the door, you stand on the doorknob and swing to the other wall.

No, let's go see some stars instead.

I knew they wouldn't let us play it. I just wanted to give them ideas for more creative games than just tag.

81

Day 4*

It's breakfast time and I'm already SICK of Er-ick.

He put stickers upside down by the bunk bed ladder.

Stickers.

Smellie purseboy

So of course I step all over them.

Not too bad, but when you need to run a half mile to the bathroom in the morning, seconds count.

And that's not all . . .

He ties my shoes together with tight knots.

And short-laces one side on each.

Plus he keeps trying to grab this book.

Aunt Ug says we all smell ripe and we have to take showers NOW. So, where to hide this book . . .

*Nobody peed on me overnight. Thank goodness.

IDEAS: Where to hide it

duct tape

No, no, no!!!
My duffel bag is the
FIRST place he'll look!

Ahh, nice shower. I come back to get my book and find this:

wet hair

My book is right where I left it.

NO FROGS!
Who would do this?
And did they see my book??
More important, did they read it?

I don't mind having Tiffie go with me. In fact, I think I prefer her company to everyone else's. Hey, maybe I can mold her into someone better!

These are rules for life. Use them for good and not for evil:

- Have courage.
- Learn from the past.
- Respect the earth.
- Play lots of games.
- Don't drink a lot of liquids before bedtime.
- Don't worry so much about what you look like.
- Your family is strange. Save yourself by not getting too close to them.
- Always look for an exit route.
- Remember the ant song.

Tiffie is a very good student. She repeats each point. And she sings the ant song for me. She memorized it in just 3 days!

She reminds me of myself at her age.

I showed her some stuff in the woods.

Poison ivy vines grow up trees

Poison ivy

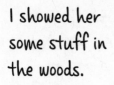

if it has leaves of three, let it be

red stem where the leaves join it

Praying mantis

Females try to eat the males. They bite their heads off! Disgusting. But it's nice to see females get a-head sometimes.
    ha ha

Bear tracks

same size as Tiffie's hand

Yikes! We have to be careful!

While Tiffie catches AND RELEASES frogs at the pond, I ponder the mystery of who emptied the frog containers.

Uncle Ewing
Aunt Ug
Deanna
Tiffie
} ?
Maybe
?

Me
Er-ick
Ben-Ben
} No—
didn't,
wouldn't,
or couldn't.

Whoever did it deserves an award because it SAVED all those frogs.

The Freedom Frog Award
For humanitarian and frogitarian services to our web-footed amphibian pals.

F.F.A.

Oh, ICK.
Look who's here.

I just finished convincing Tiffie that it's bad to
catch and keep frogs if you can't give them a
good home, and here's Er-ick. He must have seen
that the frogs were set free.

Writing this later—
It all happened so fast.

And it only gets worse.

So I jab a bigger stick at him, and hit him in the face, and he yells and yanks on it and then . . .

He pulls ME in!
It is HORRIBLE.
Absolutely AWFUL.

The smell—
like decomposing
liver being boiled
in a vat.

The feel—
like thick syrup
all over you.
Warm, like a
boatload of
elephants
peed in it.

The taste—
oh my gosh, I wish
I could forget it.
Like eating putrid
mildew that's been
fermenting for a
thousand years.

I freak out. Anyone would!

And I swear I could feel something
pulling on my shoes.

It was
TERRIFYING.

Fear turns to rage: He pulled me in on purpose, I know it!

Suddenly I WANT to push him nder so Seaweed Sally can get him.

But I concentrate on getting myself out. I'm pulling on the grass with all my might, my arms are sore, my fingers are almost bleeding from grasping at anything . . .

Suddenly I feel myself getting pushed onto the edge of the grass. It's adrenaline, I'm sure. People get bursts of superhuman strength when they're pushed to their limits.

I am superhuman!

Er-ick is throwing up on the grass (so am I).
I pull his hat out for him. It's not too slimy,
surprisingly. Tiffie is still all upset about
Seaweed Sally.

Then Er-ick starts running. At first I don't
know what's going on, and then it occurs to me:
The LAKE! I run too.

Higgins Lake is freezing cold because of all the rain we've had.

And it's super clear and not very deep.

The waves come in, bringing in little fishes and bits of driftwood, and the waves go out, taking bits of pond scum.

We stay in the water a long time, coughing and snorting and wheezing. I try to get all the algae out of my hair and my clothes—impossible.

Finally we walk back to camp without talking.

Holy cow. HE helped me out? When I didn't have any more strength, I felt something boost me up onto the grass. That was HIM? Courage and generosity? In Er-ick? Is that possible?

Why did you help me get out?

DUH! I had no choice! You were in my way so I had to push you out first.

We still get punished. We have to go to the hospital and cough up some gunk for the doctors to study to make sure we don't have some horrid pond scum disease now. Bleah.

Even worse, Aunt Ug makes us promise to be nicer to each other and quit the name-calling.

I have to think about all this.

I take another shower—
my third today. I still
don't feel clean.

Late dinner: FISH.
And spinach that
looks like seaweed.
It's disgusting.
I can't eat.

After dinner we
have a campfire.
Er-ick is pretty
quiet, like me.

I'm sitting where most of the smoke will blow into my face. I know it's weird, but it feels better to be in the smoke, like it's burning all the pond germs and scum out of me.

Ugh.

No matter how many times I swish water in my mouth and spit it out, I can still taste that frog algae.

Later, in the cabin. . .
Uncle Ewing says ten minutes until lights out.

I know what I have to do:
I have to go back to the frog pond.

It's like getting back up on a horse after it throws you.

I don't want to, though.

Day 5

I dream a bunch of frogs are holding me hostage until Er-ick promises not to capture any more of them. Which of course he won't promise. Then he morphs into a praying mantis and I wake up smiling.

While we are doing the breakfast dishes I ask Tiffie to go with me to see the frogs again.

By the time we're on the trail to the pond, everyone wants to go.

OPERATION POND RECONCILIATION

I am not afraid. I am not afraid.

my mantra

It's like a detective show. We locate the log Er-ick fell off of, and the sticks I used to try to save him, and our sunken footprints and handprints in the muck.

It's just a pond. Not very big. Maybe not even very deep. I survived it and I'm not afraid of it anymore.

I catch a frog, pet it, and let it go in the swampy water.

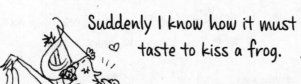

Suddenly I know how it must taste to kiss a frog.

Handsome prince or not, I think I would decline.

Ew!

We go to the lake and Tiffie says we should make a giant sand frog in honor of our pond adventure, so we do. And we tell every silly frog joke we could think of.

Q: How deep should we dig the frog?
A: Knee-deep, knee-deep!

Q: What is a frog's favorite food?
A: French flies!

Q: Why are frogs so happy?
A: Because they EAT whatever bugs them!

Q: What animal has more lives than a cat?
A: A frog! He croaks every night.

Q: What do you call a frog who crosses the road, jumps in a mud puddle, and crosses over the road again?
A: A dirty double-crosser!

⋀ this means sacrificial animal

Then we wade in the lake, gathering the best rocks and shells.

this book

Minnows
They're so cute!
They dart around your
feet. I catch a minnow
with my bare hands—
you have to be FAST.

We put the rocks and shells around the giant sand frog to protect him.

LUNCH

Leftovers:
- Tacos (from Dead Frog Night)
- Fish (from Pond Scum Night)
- Hot dogs (from Only Creeps Pick on Tiffie Night)

Er . . . I think I'll have a peanut butter sandwich instead.

After lunch, we get to swim!

Things I like to do at the beach:
- Walk on my hands in the water.
  - Bury my toes in the cold sand under the water.

- Get my legs all messy with sand, and then lift them up and watch the sand slide off.
- Keep really still so the minnows think I'm a rock and swim near me.

minnows

(actual size)

I also like to walk on my knees so the water is right below my chin, and see how far I can go before the water hits my mouth.

I like to pretend I'm the sole survivor of the *Titanic* and see how long I can float on my back (a long time, which is why I am the sole survivor).

I like to run in the deeper water—I like how hard it is to move my legs, and the sound of the water WHOOSHing as I stride through it.

supermodel on a photo shoot

I like to shoot straight up out of the water like a rocket, as high up as I can go.

Mostly I like to be by myself at the beach (but not always).

I like getting buried in the sand and watching cracks form all over me as I slowwwly get up.

Yikes!
Earthquake!

Sand castles are pretty good, giant frogs are better, and sand snowmen make people wonder if aliens have landed.

And this gives Deanna an idea . . .

PRANK

Deanna and I race back to camp to make a surprise for everyone else when they open the cabin door: two crazed camper dummies that we hope will make them scream like babies.

We shut the door and hide in the bushes across from the cabin. We have the perfect view, and we don't have to wait very long . . .

113

SUCCESS!

We laugh so hard our stomachs hurt.
They scream until they're hoarse. We have to give
them a chance to get over it (and maybe get even)
so we're going to rent bicycles for an hour from
the camp store.

Hiding this book at the end of my sleeping bag,
and we're outta here! (Still laughing, too!)

Who knew Deanna could be so creative?

No one likes you, either.

stink

you

I'm Ellie and
I smell bad.

OH MY GOSH OH MY GOSH OH MY GOSH!

While Deanna and I were out bike riding,
Er-ick found my book
and read it
and drew in it.

MY PRIVATE BOOK.

Could anything worse possibly happen?

No. This is just about as horrid as life gets.

Eric had this.
I believe it's yours.

this book

Me.
Run to the field.
NOW.

DAMAGE CONTROL:
Don't panic. THINK!

- How much did Er-ick read?
- Who else did he show MY BOOK to?
- Did Aunt Mug read it too?
- Can I live out here for 3 days?

YUM, DINNER!
Dandelion leaves are edible, and grasshoppers supposedly taste good compared to other bugs.

Yes, I will just live out here in the field eating bugs.

I can't BELIEVE he read my book. We were just starting to get along. He's a creep.

Things I could do:
1) Act like it never happened.
2) Tell them the whole book is just a joke.
3) Try to find out how much Er-ick read.
4) Take a bus home so I never have to face them again.

Oh, great. It gets even worse. Aunt Ug is headed this way.

Aunt Ug: Can we talk?

Me: Ulp. Uh. Yes?

Aunt Ug: I read your sketch diary.

Me: I was afraid of that.

Aunt Ug: You're very talented, Ellie.

Me: Huh?

Aunt Ug: You have a powerful voice and you're a natural leader. The other kids really look up to you.

Me: (blinking, this isn't what I expected to hear)

Aunt Ug: Did you know I was an artist when I was your age?

Me: You were??

She's nothing like an artist now.

Turns out Aunt Ug wanted to be a spy and an artist, but her parents thought she should be a secretary and then a wife and mom, so she gave up her dreams.

And you're not the first to call me Ug, either. Or to mention my spitting.

I feel my face turn red. I don't know what to say.

And then she says this:
"You know, seeing you draw all weekend makes me want to get back into my art."
Wow.
My brain is in slow motion.
Aunt Mug as an artist?
No way. Well, maybe as a grumpy, depressed one, painting the *Moaning Lisa*.

Whistler's Mother would be *Spittler's Mother*. Ha!

Ellie, I know you haven't had an easy time with our family. But I appreciate that you've been a good influence on Tiffie.

Uh.

I think if you give the rest of us a chance, you'll find we're not your enemies.

You might even find we have something in common—like how you and I both like to draw. Speaking of which, maybe I will draw YOU sometime.

Draw me?

Sure. Artists only draw things they care about.

I finally get up the guts to ask her:
How much of my book did Eric read?

Probably all of it. He's a
fast reader. Plus it's an
interesting subject—HIMSELF.

Then she drops
the bombshell:

Ellie, I think you need to find Eric.
This is too big to ignore for three
days, and I don't like how you two
have been fighting all this week.

Okay.

Then she leaves.
This was a good talk at first. I'm not real happy
with how it ends.

I am a nice girl.

People like me at school.

I'm not rude to people usually.

I don't pull the wings off insects,

I don't hurt little kids on purpose,

I hold doors for old ladies.

I even apologize to chairs if I bump into them!

I don't steal things.

I don't wreck things.

In fact, I tried to save Eric's life!

I'm just normal.

SO WHY DO I
FEEL SO GUILTY?

Your Honor, I intend to prove the defendant is sssneaky.

Proceed.

She's SLIMY.

She's CRABBY.

Instead of doing the right thing, she turns CHICKEN!

Verdict: GUILTY!
Punishment: Operation Apology

1. Buy a candy bar at the camp store to use as bait.
2. Apologize to Er-ick the dung beetle (and he'd better apologize too).

I want to punch him in the mouth.

Okay, new tactic: Appeal to his sense of logic.

Look, you torpid sloth, if I were to let the frogs go, it would be on the last day so you couldn't go back and get more!

Speaking of which, you should be grateful because I saved your stupid hat!

For your information, it's a FEDORA, not a "hat." And YOU should be grateful I saved your stupid YOU!

Well, I AM!

So we agree! You're stupid!

This is so not going well.

Okay, deep breath. Trying again.

Er-ick, you could stop being such a pain and listen for once. I'm being nice and you're acting like a 3-year-old.

Oops. I must have hit a nerve. He explodes.

You think you're so smart, spying on everyone and acting like you're better than we are. You're a LOSER and a LIAR and you SMELL.

Great. So much for Operation Apology. All I did was make the warthog angry.

Ha! We have a little more in common than I thought.

FINALLY an agreement.

We lay out our arsenal and decide on a strategy: disappearing ink spitballs.

ERIC'S AUTOMATIC SPITBALL MACHINE USING A CHEAP MECHANICAL PENCIL:

① Unscrew tip and throw away.

② Pull eraser part out until it breaks loose.

③ Break off tip.

shaft

cylinder

clip

④ Break off end so cylinder is uniformly straight.

⑤ Loop rubber band around eraser.

shaft

⑥ Put rubber band and eraser back into eraser hole, and put shaft back into cylinder.

⑦ Loop other end of rubber band around clip, maybe twist it a few times.

⑧ To load it:

pull back cylinder

push in spitball that's been dipped in disappearing ink

⑨ Let go of eraser. It will spring back and launch a blue spitball.

132

I decide to quit drawing Eric as a monster, in an effort to get along.

Our plan works! Only one problem . . .

Deanna is a total snitch.

And Aunt Mug
still spits when
she yells.

134

They say:
- we're a bad influence on the other kids,
- disappearing ink doesn't always disappear from clothing,
- this is the stupidest stunt they ever saw,
- we have to do the dishes for the rest of the trip,
- no more pranks,
- any more fights or complaints and we're grounded to our bunks for the rest of the trip, and
- spitballs are disgusting and could be dangerous and there is zero tolerance for them.

neck turns red

Yikes. Damage control time.

When they're done I stand up and repeat back to them what they just said (an old trick I learned from Risa and Josh). This technique always works. They realize I was listening and it prevents more lecturing.

It was a stupid stunt, we won't do any more pranks, and we're sorry for being a bad influence.

At dinner I make a list with everyone. This is our last night at camp and we have to do something truly great.

- ☐ bear hunt (no way—I'll sing the bear hunt song, but I'm not hunting)
- ☐ play sardines
- ☐ nature walk (without parents)
- ☐ go to bed early

  Oh thank you so much for that suggestion, Aunt Mug!

- ☐ wash the van

  Another great suggestion, courtesy of Uncle Ewing.

  Maybe we should make this list where grown-ups can't hear us . . .

- ☐ get kids from other campsites together for a giant hide-and-seek game
- ☐ catch some frogs

  Uh, no.

- ☐ take Ben-Ben to the playground

  Be responsible for the monkey boy? NO WAY.

  We gotta get out of here FAST.

CHOOSING WHO IS "IT"

Say a rhyme while tapping each shoe around the circle. Whoever you land on last is out.

The last shoe left in the circle is "it" for the game.

Train, train, number 9, coming down Chicago line, if the train should jump the track, do you want your money back? Yes, no, or maybe so? Y-E-S spells yes and you are not "it!"

yes

Eric
Deanna
Tiffie
me

Bubble gum, bubble gum, in the dish, how many pieces do you wish?

5

One—two—three—four—five and you are not "it!"

My mother, your mother, live across the street. 18-19 Broadway Street. Every night they have a fight and this is what they say:
Acka backa soda cracker, acka backa boo. Acka backa soda cracker, out goes YOU!

I am "it."

138

We play SARDINES.

I LOVE this game.

It's like the opposite of hide and seek.

The person who is "it" hides and everyone else tries to find him.

When you find him, you quietly crawl in and hide there too.

Pretty soon you have a whole bunch of giggling friends all squeezed into one little space.

The last person to find "it" loses the game and the first person to find "it" is the new "it" for the next game.

This is my best place to hide.
But Eric accidentally sits on Tiffie's head. Oops.

We decide to go on a nature hike. Our inventory:

Eric's Boy Scout knife	my mini first-aid kit	Deanna's watch
my book on survival in the wild	my compass	Deanna's granola bar and two dollars
my bandana	Ben-Ben's head lamp flashlight (he won't know—he's asleep)	Tiffie's water bottle on a belt
a box of cereal—snack-size Sugar Blaster O's	Deanna's sweatband	my book and pen
		Eric's empty water balloons (8)
Eric's stash of candy, which we promise not to eat unless we get really desperate	my book of animal tracks	8 eyes 8 ears 8 hands 8 feet

Eric wants to see a bear.
I'd prefer something less ferocious.

First order of business: A symbol for good luck on our path. ♣

This is so cool. It's like we own the forest. The trees bow to our will.

A rabbit!

Bats!

We find a chipmunk that takes cereal right out of Eric's hand (but ONLY his).

Rabbits are too scared of us to even come near. Too bad—no cereal for them!

Tiffie's picking dandelions for Aunt Mug. We see:

daisies   black-eyed   Queen   Dandelions   Indian
           Susans   Anne's lace   blankets

We find a branch that bends over the path like a bench. It's very comfortable!

Wintergreen! Shiny green leaves. Tear a leaf and smell it—it smells like gum!

about 4 inches

Diving to catch bugs. They ignore the cereal we throw.

Tie the tops of saplings together and throw a poncho over it to make a little house.

We could LIVE out here!

my bandana

Bad news: Fern stems rip your hand if you try to pick them. Tiffie finds out the hard way. OUCH!
Cold water from her water bottle helps.

To cheer her up we start singing camp songs.
Deanna starts this: Twinkle, twinkle, little star,
            how we wonder where we are.
I add: We just want to find our way,
        to our camp before it's day.
Eric wrecks it with: Twinkle, twinkle, take us home,
cuz this is a goofy poem.

 I'm hungry and we ate all the candy already.

Okay, fine. They're badger tracks. Good job
making me feel stupid, Deanna.

Tiffie asked what we would do if it WAS a bear,
and I pulled out my survival book:

> Bears are most dangerous when they're hungry or with
> their cubs. If attacked, fall to the ground and roll into a
> ball, protecting your neck. Play dead. If a bear attacks
> you in your tent, fight back. Aim for the eyes and nose.

Take that, Deanna.

And for a mountain lion, you make a lot of noise and wave your jacket so you look bigger. Fight back aggressively,

aiming for the eyes and mouth. Protect your neck and throat because that's how they kill their prey.

Eric: If I see a bear out here, I'm running.

Me: The book says not to! You can't outrun a bear!

Eric: I don't have to outrun the bear. I only have to outrun YOU. Ha ha ha ha!

Me: Grrrrr.

Tiffie: I'm thirsty and I'm out of water.

Me: Bite the tip of your tongue. That's an old Girl Scout trick.

Eric: Put a clean pebble in your mouth. Old Boy Scout trick.

Tiffie: Which one should I do?

Deanna: Pebble. Biting your tongue will hurt—duh!

Me: No! Bite your tongue! You don't bite it HARD. Duh!

Deanna: Two against one. We win. Right, Eric?

Deanna: Where IS Eric?

All roads lead to Rome, my dad always says.
Well, I hope not! We want HOME, not Rome. I
decide to make up a song:

> This is the path that never ends.
> Yes, it goes on and on, my friends.
> Some people started walking it
> Not knowing where it led
> And they'll continue walking it
> Forever 'til they're DEAD.
> This is the path that never ends . . .
> (repeats)

Hmm. I guess we should look for him.

We shout until our throats hurt. And we don't have any water.

Where is he?

My survival book is no help for this. I admit it—I'm getting worried.

This compass is useless, too.
It points in directions, sure. But we want it to point the way out of here.

← A more useful compass

What should we do?
We can't go home without him.

Mom and Dad would kill us.

What if a bear got him?

Or Seaweed Sally?

I'm scared.

If we ever find him I'm going to be nice to him.

Do you think he's dead?

I don't know.

:(Let's keep looking for him.

This next part happens fast.

Eric jumps out from behind a tree.

RAH!

Startled, Tiffie trips over a tree stump.

She cuts her shin.
And twists her ankle.
Cheezers.
No water to clean it.
No extra bandana.
Deanna doesn't want her precious sweatband to get blood on it.

So I donate my sock as a bandage.

Yes, that's spit.

RULES:

1. No more separating from the group.
2. No more getting hurt.

My arms and back are aching.
Did I only carry her for 7 minutes?
It felt like 100.

Deanna's watch is handy. I only get to write in
this book when we rest, after 3 carries.

It's getting too dark to see,
and Eric's stingy with
the flashlight.
    Which, by the way,
    is growing dim.

Two more
minutes.

8:45p.m.:
New problem:
We saw a big elk
and had to go off
the trail to get
around him. He's
chewing something.
Maybe his last victim.

Now we can't find the trail.

9:00 p.m.:
Deanna says we should plan to sleep out here.
I say that would be dangerous.
We're fighting over what's best.
My arms hurt.
Tiffie's crying.

9:20 p.m.:
We can't carry Tiffie 7 minutes. It's 5 minutes now,
then we switch. The flashlight's fading fast. Tiffie
put her bouquet inside her water bottle so she won't
have to carry it. She's a smart little kid.

Dad & Mom, I love you! ← just in case we don't make
it back

9:31 p.m.:
It's hard walking and carrying Tiffie.
Spiderwebs stretch across my face—creepy!
Sometimes I can feel something crawling on my
neck but can't scratch it because my arms
are full of Tiffie.

Witchy tree branches
pull at us,
ripping my
shirt. I have
a thousand
scratches
on me.

9:39 p.m.:
Deanna and Tiffie are yelling for help.
Maybe a ranger will hear us. Or at
least it'll keep the bears away.

I'm thirsty. My legs itch.
Flashlight's almost gone.

Are we gonna die out here?

If someone finds this book,
know that we tried our best.
Give my book collection
to Amy, my best friend.

Written later:
While carrying Tiffie I have an idea: We all stay super
quiet and see if we can identify any sounds or smells to
help us figure out where we are, or how to get out of
the woods. We hear crackling and owls and insect
sounds—but—
WAHOO! We also hear frogs!
We follow the sound to THE POND!
But it doesn't look like the pond we know, especially
in the moonlight.

But then Eric finds the symbol I put there earlier, made with sticks.

It means "Group desires a peaceful relation"— I put it there to apologize for the big dead bullfrog.

WHAT A RELIEF!!!

From the frog pond it's easy to get back to the cabin. Easier to see, too, because no trees block the moon. We run part of the way.

10:00 p.m.:
Aunt Mug starts crying when we walk into camp.
Uncle Ewing looks stunned (kind of, it's hard to tell
with him).
The rangers look happy at least.

Aunt Mug looks like
she just rode a
merry-go-round
upside down.

I let Aunt Mug and Uncle Ewing read my book (just the woods adventure) and they let us stay up at the campfire for a while.

After an ice pack on her ankle, burn cream on her hand, and bandages for her cuts, Tiffie will be okay.

Now that we're safe and warm with snacks, we're thinking this was a pretty cool last night at camp. We can't stop talking about it.

We made it out of the woods because we all worked together. But I wasn't REALLY scared.

Well, maybe a little.

Okay, time to clear up a mystery . . .

So who set the frogs free?

Huh? I thought YOU did, Ellie!

Maybe I can help . . .

THE NEWT STORY

I tell them about my mom and Aunt Mug's two newts. I've heard the story a hundred times.

They kept them in a giant pickle jar.

floating rocks

pump

One time they discovered one of the newts was super fat.

aerator ball

tube

It turned out the aerator ball had come off the tube, so the tube sent a lot of big air bubbles into the water and the newt swallowed them.

Grandpa had to rub the newt really carefully so it could burp out all the air.

Aunt Mug laughs (that's a very good sign).

Day 6

It's freezing outside, which makes it easier to accept that we're ending camp today.

Still, I don't want to go home. Ha! I never thought I'd feel that way.

(annoyed)

Funny how last night was so miserable but now we're having fun talking about it.

We have a ton of stuff to pack up.

Load the van.
Clean the cabin.
Get on the road
after lunch.

Good-bye, Higgins Lake! I'm sad to leave.

We played the Alphabet Game once we hit the highway.

To play:

On signs and license plates, find a word that starts with an A, then a B, then a C . . .

The first person to find every letter from A to Z wins.

No doubles: If one person finds an E, like on an exit sign, nobody else can use that E on that sign.

My family always plays the Alphabet Game on long car trips, and I always lose because I'm slower to see things. But with these guys, I have a fighting chance!

After the Alphabet Game, we play the Question Game. Hold a normal conversation, but everything has to be a question.

And it goes on and on . . .

We get to Aunt Mug's house in time for dinner (pizza, yum) and unpack the van and put everything away.

Mom and Dad are coming tomorrow at noon to get me. I'm kind of happy about that (I'll be able to call Scott) and kind of sad. I sort of felt like triplets with Eric and Deanna.

I'm thinking it might be cool to spend more ti—
　　　　　　Whoa!

WATER
BALLOONS!

This means **WAR!** Ben-Ben is pelting me with water balloons. Eric must have put him up to it! Quick—must hide the book.

Writing this later . . .

Eric and Ben-Ben have pails full of water balloons (COLD water, too), and sneak up on each of us girls.

BUT WE GET THEM BACK!

First we run inside. Of course they think we're tattling on them—but we are really putting this book out of the line of fire and filling Deanna's stash of water balloons.

SPLAT!!

We catch them completely off guard.

Garbage can lids for shields don't help them very much.

But Ben-Ben is the sneaky little stealth blaster, fearlessly running under the line of fire and splashing us with cups of water. Then he grabs the garden hose . . . I'm laughing so hard. We're all soaking wet by the time Aunt Mug calls us inside.

Deanna, Tiffie, and I sleep in the living room, like a slumber party.

I had a lot more fun with you guys than I thought I would.

Well, we had more fun with YOU than we thought we would!

Hmm. That doesn't sound like a compliment. But I'll ignore it. Good night. ☺
(I have 24 mosquito bites just on one ankle.)

Day 7

Aunt Mug takes us to an art store. I LOVE
ART STORES!
She buys paints for herself.
And sketchbooks!

For her, Tiffie, Eric, and ME.

She says there are two
rules for my sketchbook:
1. Have fun with it.
2. If I ever have a problem,
talk about it instead of
keeping it to myself.

I think I can manage that.

Next we go to the pet store to get Eric and
Deanna some newts.

They're soooo cute.
(the newts, I mean)

Back to Aunt Mug's house just in time . . .

 How's my girl?

We missed you! I hope you had a good time with your cousins.

I had a great time!

Still, it's nice to go home.

So, what did you learn?

THINGS I'VE LEARNED

1) Things aren't always as they seem.
2) You can't judge a book by its cover, or a vacation by its first day, or the value of a camping trip by whether it's in a tent.
3) Eric isn't so bad, I guess.
4) The monkey boy is smarter and more fun than I thought. Actually, my cousins are too.
5) If things aren't working out, be patient. It'll change (just like Michigan weather).
6) Elk are not meat eaters but they're still awfully scary.
7) Carrying a 7-year-old through a pine forest is quite a big job.
8) Spying is cool, but you should expect to get caught.
9) No girl is an island. We're all in this together. Might as well try to get along.
10) Eating bugs is overrated.

Mom said there are more surprises coming this summer.

One thing's for sure: I'll need lots of sketchbooks!

Turn the page for exciting Ellie extras:

An Interview with the Author

How to Keep a Sketch Journal

How to Sketch

Tips for Drawing Comics

An Interview with the Author

I started keeping an almost-daily sketch journal when I was fifteen. A beloved teacher gave me a blank book to start in. I drew a lot and was usually dissatisfied with what I drew. But I kept trying to do my best.

The people around me—now and when I was young—are the inspiration for the cast of characters in my Ellie books.

"Ellie Math":

How did you get started in kids' books?

I was born into a huge, creative family.

me

Our house was crowded but never dull. April Fools' Day and Halloween were especially entertaining. I drew and wrote a lot. I told everyone I was going to be rich and famous someday but most people laughed it off. I felt misunderstood and confused growing up. I had some rough times. Maybe everyone does.

Journaling helped me sort things out as a kid. And it still does as a grown-up!

Over the years I have created hundreds of sketch journals. I even won a bunch of contests with them.

I went off to college and studied
a million things (but not much art).

I landed a cool job doing advertising
and newspaper art at the university.

I married and had four kids (who are
all great friends!).

I kept sketching and journaling all that time. Then
a few years ago, some writer friends suggested I try
writing a children's book in my sketchbook style.
And that's how Ellie
McDoodle was born.

> What was your favorite part of creating Ellie's story?

There were two favorite parts:
1) The affirmation I felt when my agent and some very respected editors said they loved the book.
2) Working on revisions.

I spent many, many days reworking the art and text. I racked my brain trying to make the book better, and I listened nonstop to reruns of my favorite funny TV shows. It was very hard work, but I loved every minute of it!

What advice do you have for young people wanting to become artists or writers?

Read, read, read. Anything you can get your hands on.

Draw, draw, draw. Don't get discouraged.

Open your brain to new activities, new sights, and new experiences. It'll give you something to write about.

Keep a journal, any kind.

Show your work to people you trust— teachers, librarians . . . they can help you find resources.

Be yourself. The world doesn't need more copies of things. It needs more YOU.

How to Keep a Sketch Journal

1. Take a test run. Go outside with a piece of paper and a pencil. Be quiet for a couple of minutes and just observe the things around you. What do you sense?

   What do you see?

   What do you feel?

   What do you hear?

   What do you smell?

   What do you taste?

2. How big or small is what you see?
   How can you measure it?

About 6 inches — dollar

2 cm — nickel

1½ inches? (thumb)

1 foot tall (bottle)

8½" — standard paper sheet — 11

8½" — angle of folded edge = 12" — 11

3. How much can you say in words, and how much can you show in pictures? It's okay to use phrases and lists instead of whole sentences. Interesting words are more fun to read:

   crackle - flurry - gleaming - smudge - grin
   leap - sparkle - grimy - rumble - chirping

4. Things to add to your journal:

-maps
-games
-animals you see
-words you love
-draw your friends

-draw your inventions
-list your favorite
  things
-stuff to remember

How to Sketch

Snail

At the zoo:

African pygmy goats are mostly triangles and rectangles

Mandrills look like cartoons!

Try to see SHAPES in everything. Even the most complex objects are really just a bunch of simple shapes. Can you see the shapes in these images? Make it easy on yourself: use shapes to start your own images. First draw the shapes lightly in pencil, then fill in the details. The more you practice, the easier it gets.

Decide on a focal point—a spot in the scene that you want the viewer to notice the most. Put the most detail or the most interesting color in that spot.

Focal point

Hint: Don't put the focal point in the exact center of the page. That's boring.

Only show the most important details. Keep it simple.

Color: use colored pencils, crayons, markers, or paint. Or just use a regular pencil and label the color.

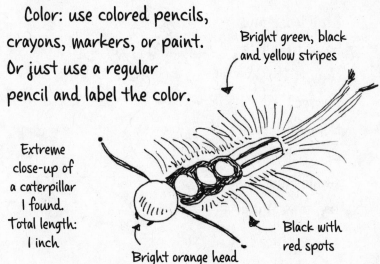

Bright green, black and yellow stripes

Extreme close-up of a caterpillar I found. Total length: 1 inch

Bright orange head

Black with red spots

How to draw me

Stay loose and have fun. It's okay if it isn't perfect. Nobody draws perfectly every single time they try something.

How to draw Er-ick

lots of grabby arms

Ben-Ben is harder to draw because he never stands still to model!

Don't forget to add his missing sock and shoe, far away from his feet!

Tips for Drawing Comics

Balloons — First: write the words. Last: draw voice balloons around the words.

Action — Action keeps the reader's attention.

Shortcuts
- Tracing paper makes it easy to redraw your art.
- Copy comics you love. Give them your own twist, your own style.

Have Fun — Make sure you have fun! Frustration means it's probably time to quit for a while.

"U" Laugh — Make "U"rself laugh. It's hard to make everyone laugh. So start by making yourself laugh!

Keep It Simple, Sweetie — If it's too complicated, it's hard to create and hard for your readers to understand.

Don't miss Ellie's next adventure!

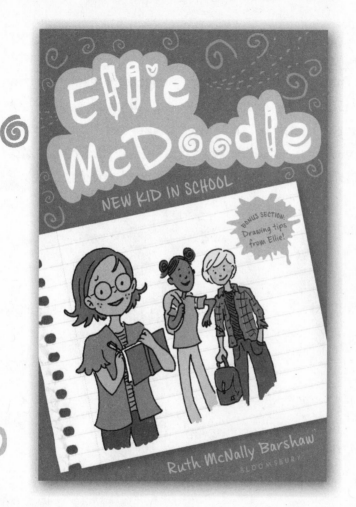

When Ellie moves to a new town and a new school, she gets the new-kid-blues. The kids at Ellie's new school aren't very welcoming and even the teachers can't remember her name. But when the students need someone to lead their rally against long lunch lines (and bad food), Ellie is on the case. Will better lunches lead to new friends?

RUTH McNALLY BARSHAW, lifelong writer and artist, has worked in the advertising field, illustrated for newspapers, and won numerous essay-writing contests. She lives in Lansing, Michigan, with her family. Ruth is also the author of Ellie's other adventures, including her latest, *Ellie McDoodle: Most Valuable Player*. Visit her at www.ruthexpress.com.